A Note to Parents and Caregivers:

Read-it! Joke Books are for children who are moving ahead on the amazing road to reading. These fun books support the acquisition and extension of reading skills as well as a love of books.

Published by the same company that produces *Read-it!* Readers, these books introduce the question/answer and dialogue patterns that help children expand their thinking about language structure and book formats.

When sharing joke books with a child, read in short stretches. Pause often to talk about the meaning of the jokes. The question/answer and dialogue formats work well for this purpose and provide an opportunity to talk about the language and meaning of the jokes. Have the child turn the pages and point to the pictures and familiar words. When you read the jokes, have fun creating the voices of characters or emphasizing some important words. Be sure to reread favorite jokes.

There is no right or wrong way to share books with children. Find time to read with your child, and pass on the legacy of literacy.

Adria F. Klein, Ph.D.
Professor Emeritus
California State University
San Bernardino, California

Editor: Jill Kalz
Designer: Joe Anderson
Page Production: Melissa Kes
Creative Director: Keith Griffin
Editorial Director: Carol Jones
The illustrations in this book were created digitally.

Picture Window Books
5115 Excelsior Boulevard
Suite 232
Minneapolis, MN 55416
877-845-8392
www.picturewindowbooks.com

Printed in the United States of America.

Library of Congress Cataloging-in-Publication Data
Donahue, Jill L.
How do you get there? : a book of transportation jokes / by Jill L. Donahue ;
illustrated by Amy Bailey Muehlenhardt.
p. cm. — (Read-it! joke books—supercharged!)
Includes bibliographical references and index.
ISBN-13: 978-1-4048-2367-9 (hardcover)
ISBN-10: 1-4048-2367-0 (hardcover)
1. Transportation—Juvenile humor. 2. Riddles, Juvenile. I. Muehlenhardt, Amy Bailey,
1974– II. Title. III. Series.
PN6231.T694D66 2007
818'.602—dc22   2006003405

Read-it! Joke Books
Supercharged!
Orange Level

How Do You Get There?

A Book of Transportation Jokes

by Jill L. Donahue

illustrated by Amy Bailey Muehlenhardt

Special thanks to our advisers for their expertise:

Adria F. Klein, Ph.D.
Professor Emeritus, California State University
San Bernardino, California

Susan Kesselring, M.A.
Literacy Educator
Rosemount–Apple Valley–Eagan (Minnesota) School District

PiCTURE WiNDOW BOOKS
Minneapolis, Minnesota

How do rabbits travel?
By hareplane.

On what kinds of ships do good students sail?
Scholarships.

What kind of train gives people colds?
A choo-choo train.

What bus crossed the ocean?
Columbus.

Why did the driver throw her pocket change on the road?
She wanted to stop on a dime.

What kind of pool can't you swim in?
A car pool.

What kind of car can drive over water?
Any kind of car, if it uses a bridge.

Where did the angler go to catch an airplane?
The jet stream.

What kind of truck is always a "he" and never a "she"?
A "male" truck.

What would you call the life story of a car?
An autobiography.

What is a banged-up used car called?
A car in first-crash condition.

What did one windshield wiper say to the other windshield wiper when it couldn't make up its mind?
"Stop going back and forth!"

What kinds of boats do vampires take?
Blood vessels.

What lives under the sea and carries a lot of people?
An octobus.

What do British whales eat?

Fish and ships.

What is left on the ground after it rains cats and dogs?

Rain poodles.

What zooms up the river?
A motorpike.

What happened when the frog's car broke down?
It was "toad" away.

Where do astronauts leave their spaceships?
At parking meteors.

Which driver doesn't need a license?
A screwdriver.

What goes through towns and up and over hills but doesn't move?

A road.

Why did the man put an extra muffler on his car?

He wanted it to stay warm in the cold weather.

Where do old Volkswagens go?

To the old Volks home.

Why did the starfish cross the road?
   To get to the other tide.

What does the mechanic charge to fix a tire?
   A flat rate.

What kind of monkey can fly?
   A hot-air baboon.

What kinds of stories does a ship's captain like to tell?

"Ferry" tales.

What is the difference between a train and a teacher?

The train says, "Choo, choo," while a teacher says, "Spit out that gum."

Why couldn't the couple play cards while they were on the cruise ship?

Someone was always sitting on the deck.

What did one elevator say to the other?

"I think I'm coming down with something."

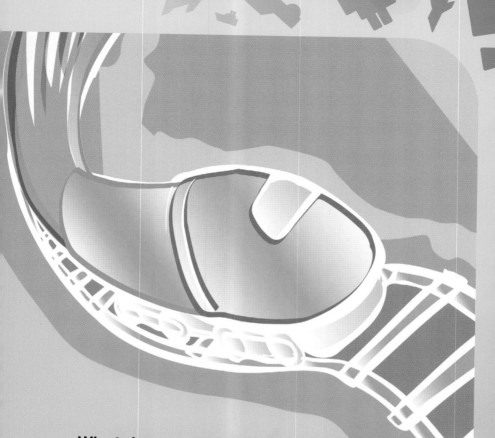

What do you get when you cross a gun with a locomotive?

A bullet train.

How are an airline pilot and a football player alike?

They both want nice, safe touchdowns.

What kind of ship never sinks?
Friendship.

What kinds of streets do ghosts haunt?
Dead ends.

DEAD END

What has one horn and gives milk?
A milk truck.

Why are astronauts successful people?
Because they always shoot for the stars.

If athletes get athlete's foot, what do astronauts get?
Missiletoe.

What should you do if you stub your toe?
Call a "toe" truck.

What do you get if you cross a spaceship with a magician?
A flying sorcerer.

What comes with a car, goes with a car, and is no use to the car—yet the car won't go without it?

Noise.

Why do birds fly south?

It's too far to walk.

What do you call a ship that attacks lambs?

A battlesheep.

What do you get when you cross a convertible with an elephant?

A cool car with a big trunk.

When does the cart come before the horse?

In the dictionary.

What do you get when you cross some strawberries with an intersection?
A traffic jam.

What is a locomotive?
A crazy reason for doing something.

Read-it! Joke Books— Supercharged!

Chitchat Chuckles: A Book of Funny Talk 1-4048-1160-5

Creepy Crawlers: A Book of Bug Jokes 1-4048-0627-X

Fur, Feathers, and Fun! A Book of Animal Jokes 1-4048-1161-3

Lunchbox Laughs: A Book of Food Jokes 1-4048-0963-5

Mind Knots: A Book of Riddles 1-4048-1162-1

Nutty Names: A Book of Name Jokes 1-4048-1163-X

Roaring with Laughter: A Book of Animal Jokes 1-4048-0628-8

Sit! Stay! Laugh! A Book of Pet Jokes 1-4048-0629-6

Wacky Workers: A Book of Job Jokes 1-4048-1164-8

What's Up, Doc? A Book of Doctor Jokes 1-4048-1165-6

Artful Antics: A Book of Art, Music, and Theater Jokes
    1-4048-2363-8

Family Follies: A Book of Family Jokes 1-4048-2362-X

*Laughing Letters and Nutty Numerals: A Book of Jokes About
    ABCs and 123s* 1-4048-2365-4

What's in a Name? A Book of Name Jokes 1-4048-2364-6

Looking for a specific title or level? A complete list
of *Read-it!* Readers is available on our Web site:
www.picturewindowbooks.com